DISCARD

Because I Am Furniture

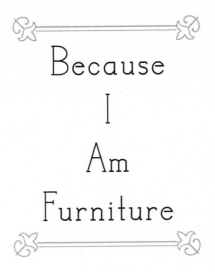

Because
I
Am
Furniture

BY

Thalia Chaltas

VIKING

VIKING

Published by Penguin Group

Penguin Group (USA) Inc., 345 Hudson Street, New York, New York 10014, U.S.A.

Penguin Group (Canada), 90 Eglinton Avenue East, Suite 700, Toronto,

Ontario, Canada M4P 2Y3 (a division of Pearson Penguin Canada Inc.)

Penguin Books Ltd, Registered Offices: 80 Strand, London WC2R 0RL, England

First published in 2008 by Viking, a member of Penguin Group (USA) Inc.

1   3   5   7   9   10   8   6   4   2

Copyright © Thalia Chaltas, 2009

LIBRARY OF CONGRESS CATALOGING-IN-PUBLICATION DATA

Chaltas, Thalia.

Because I am furniture / by Thalia Chaltas.

p. cm.

Summary: The youngest of three siblings, fourteen-year-old Anke feels both relieved and neglected because
her father abuses her brother and sister but ignores her, but when she catches him with one of her friends,
she finally becomes angry enough to take action.

ISBN 978-0-670-06298-0 (hardcover)

1. Novels in verse. 2. Child abuse—Fiction. 3. Child sexual abuse—Fiction. 4. Family problems—Fiction.
5. High schools—Fiction. 6. Schools—Fiction.] I. Title.

PZ7.5.C38Be 2009

[Fic]—dc22

2008023235

Printed in U.S.A.   Set in Egyptienne   Book design by Nancy Brennan

Only fiction and truth were used in the crafting
of this book.

To
my mother
my brother
and
my sister.

I write
now
what I could not do
then.

Because I Am Furniture

PART
ONE

I am always there.
But they don't care if I am
because I am furniture.

I don't get hit
I don't get fondled
I don't get love
because I am furniture.

Suits me fine.

When the garage door goes up
he's home.

We close up conversation
and scuttle off like crabs
each to our room—
Shut the door.
Shut the door.
Shut the door.

Mom alone in the kitchen
where she should be

before the garage door goes down
and we are locked in hell.

Dinner.

He knocked Darren onto the linoleum.

I don't remember his arm swing,
just Darren and his chair—
eight tangled limbs on the floor.

No reason that I could see.

But my father picked up his reasons and his
   plate and went
to eat
in the living room.

Darren picked up his chair and himself and we
are now eating
in customary ice-age silence.

When I was much younger
Yaicha and Darren
would point at my nose
and say,

"You don't look like us
your nose is different
you don't belong."

Yaicha and Darren
told me that I was
the mailman's child,

and I got so angry,
stalking away,
hot steam in my ribs.

Yaicha and Darren
told me that I was

the mailman's child

and now I am thinking
how wonderful it would be
to have
the mailman as
my father.

My mom.

At times I still want to
sigh,
curl into her,
nourish in her motherness,
especially
when she wears that
old suede jacket that
smells of fall leaves, like
       the pliable leather armchair
       left outside on the back porch.

But she doesn't welcome that.
Maybe I am not that young anymore.

And when he is there
all her motherness
has to be
spent on
him.

Oh, yay
charity day
visiting Angeline the Wimp.

I see her often enough at school.
Don't want to visit her house.

Since her dad
left her and her mousy mother
for some bouncy secretary in Texas
       mom and I
       are here
       to
       touch base, be friendly.
       Our moms met way back when we were
         in preschool.

Angeline irritates me—
she's delusional,
terrified,

weak.

the ocean has "man-eating seaweed"

the garden has "corn-barfing worms"

the fancy sound system has "thought-tracking
  speakers."

I didn't choose to be friends with her.

Angeline doesn't
have a father around

and my mom says she
really
needs one.

Maybe.

But
not
like
mine.

Scrubbing my volleyball knee pads
while I'm in the shower,
hot water,
way too much soap,
but, man,
three days of preseason training
on the sly
collected a hell of a stink.

The foam won't dry out overnight.

My knees will probably
froth in soap bubbles
if I dare set foot in tryouts tomorrow.

First day.
Ninth grade.
High school.

Honking in the parking lot,
upperclassmen back smacking,
squeals of recognition,
a grimly nodding principal.

I'm supposed to feel something more than just
rattled
by the sheer number of people in the halls, right?
Scared?

Except that I've been in and out of
   this building
a bunch of times for years—
         Yaicha's musicals,
         Darren's debate team.

I learned my classrooms from the map,

and I just spent whole days going to volleyball
  training here,
so I kind of get it already.

I like school.

Not scared.

But excited in that
        jiggering-on-too-much-hot-sauce
          kind of way
that it's time to
step out
of my old framework,
raw and amorphous,
to become something I've never thought of
  before.

After school is a different story.
Volleyball tryouts.

I wasn't going to do it.
Even though I crave it
I wasn't supposed to
try out
because
my father said,
"Competition is dangerous for
  a young girl's mind."

But I already like the girls from preseason
  training.
And that tenth-grader Rona saw me
growing roots
outside the locker room
dangling my new volleyball sneakers
        bought with my own money
        in secret.

Rona looked me in the eye.

"You *are* going to put on some shorts, right?"

and as she steered me
through the splintered wood door
she told me
about some player last year
who tried out with mittens on
to protect her nylon nails.

And I wasn't even nervous
because it was the same intramurals coach
from last year in eighth,
      Coach Roy,
and he had asked me to come
try out.

Passing drills
setting drills
hitting drills—
he had us try everything
with a smile
and a "one more time"
      if we didn't get it right.

I was so full in my skin,
blood pumping through,
leg muscles grinding
as I jumped and sprinted and dove.

At the end we stretched,

happy and sweaty
and on the way
to the locker room
Coach Roy said to me
"Great job!" like he did to everyone
but he meant it, too.

He looked right at me when he said it.

Swinging in the hammock,
      relaxing muscles
      heavy from tryouts,
a wild pattern
of shivering hemlock branches above me
serrating the sky.

Grasping the nearest twig
as I swing,
swing,
a few striped needles
come away
crushed
in my hand.

Inhaling their sharpness
I touch one to my tongue,
swing,
swing,
idly wondering
if this is the hemlock
people use to poison each other.

He's losing it bad tonight,
the second time this week,
chasing Yaicha out of the kitchen
holding his chair over her head—

she cowers on the living room rug.

I am close behind mom,
but it's not like I can ever do anything.

No one sees me.

Mom gets him to stop,
        with taut and twisted face, open hands,
before the chair comes down.

Yaicha runs.

He sits down, tired,
and says to mom,

"I'm sorry you had to see that."

Inevitable that he does it.

But he doesn't really want
a witness.

Lying in bed,
I am thinking that it's unfathomable,
why his anger begins
or why it ends.

There was that time
He woke us all up
at two a.m.
to go out in the street to see
the aurora borealis,

a magical flickering green spirit
dancing against the black sky
with us underneath it,
and I thought we were suddenly
a family,
woven,
peaceful.

But when we went back in
there was a raccoon in the open garage—

scuttling scared
on concrete—

and my father laughed and
shut the garage door,
roaring to send the animal
ricocheting off the rakes in the corner
in terror,
frantic for escape.

My father trapped the raccoon for the night.

Not one of us said
anything against it.

In the morning
he told Yaicha
to clean up the curling round of
raccoon shit,
cold on the
garage floor.

The foam cushions
on the old couch downstairs
disintegrate
daily
in a hush,
like each of us,

small flecks of
hardening puffs
raining mute to the floor
when I flop down to study.

And the more the couch gets used,
the less foam it keeps—

someday
just an uncomfortable
frame,
springs and other inner workings
exposed.

Silent.

Of course a full hallway.
I stub my sneaker
on the kid's heel
and we tumble like
        bowling pins,
                three of us,
    books   broadcast
            underfoot.

Dammit!

I am seventeen shades of crimson,
spitting epitaphs:

        "Here lies the girl
        whose feet grew
        their own brains
        and threw the rest of her
        over a cliff
        in front of everyone
        she'd ever known."

They call us
Nopes
>the "out" crowd,
>we don't fit their
>dog-show guidelines
>wealthy-beautiful.

We call them
Yups
>they have to
>all agree,
>yup each other
>every day on every thing.

And we say
Nope, don't
want any part
of your Yuppitude
>so tight
>society will burst
>with any change

of thought.

But being a fractured, momentary gathering
and not an actual collective,
we say
Nope
individually
with scrambled cadence

and their
Yup
is way
louder.

Those girls
over there
with Ginger Khan
know everything
about each other
        guys
        music
        toothpaste
        bra size
everything.
Look at them
huddle,
hunching their shoulders
so I can't see in.

So into themselves
they don't get it,
I don't want them
don't want
to know the day
their PMS starts,

don't want
to tell anyone
everything
about me.

"The whole *day*?" I whine.

Mom is driving with gloved fingertips.
I scraped frost off the windshield this
  morning.

"Anke, her mother may as well make the most
  of her time in Boston.
I'm sure you and Angeline will find plenty to
  do."

Right.
Me and Ange.
Whoopin' it up.

My nostrils snort
twin fog blurs on my window.

Mom glances over.
"It's Saturday, maybe Yaicha would take you

two to the mall?"

I snort again.
"Perfect, Mom.
I hate shopping,
Angeline is terrified of Yaicha,
and Yaicha is not about to agree to play
   chauffeur and babysitter."
I glare at the coming stop sign.

Mom sighs.
Honda brakes engage with rhythmic squeaks.
"Honestly, Anke. Your attitude is part of the
   problem."

I grind my teeth.
Wheels grind over gravel to a halt.
Red octagon, looming in my window.
"Sorry, Mom, but somehow I resent having a
   frickin' playdate at the age of fourteen."

Left turn onto Harper Street.

Angeline's street.

Mom taps the wheel gently with a lambskin
   thumb.

"Is she so awful, really?"

I push a breath through my lips.

Is she? Awful?

"She's fine.

But fine doesn't mean she's a friend, either."

And I don't get a choice.

"You use *that?*" Angeline squeals.

What, she's never split wood?
My shoulders are warm.
I've been at this for fifteen minutes already.

She perches on the edge of the porch to watch,
nestled in her fluffy parka
like a lost tropical bird,
knees together.

Swinging the split maul overhead,
      upper hand sliding down the shaft,
the edge lands
CRACK into the oak standing on end.

Blade stuck in the rippled grain,
I lift the whole shebang, maul and log,
and whack it on the stump base.
CRACK.

Swing,

CRACK.
Perfect thirds.

"Why don't you let Angeline try?"
How long
has my father been standing behind us?

"Oh! Oh, I don't think I could swing that
   enormous thing!"

Silently, he hands me the heavier ax,
takes mine.
Hands on Angie's hands,
he first demonstrates the swing
        as he did for me years ago,
Angie squirming, giggling.

Vessels in my heart burn,
and I turn back to my work.

Jed has wavy dark hair
eyes the ink of night
beautiful cheekbones
lean in jeans
a tilted smirk.

He lives across the street.

He says he likes me because
I just want to be friends

and I do want to be his friend
because that makes me
someone
different
from all those girls
who are dying to be more.

But no one knows
we take naps on his
damp
basement couch

after school
and sometimes he kisses me there.

It doesn't mean anything
to either one of us—
 he's a senior, after all—
but
he doesn't do it
with anyone else, either.

Final cut for volleyball,
still a mixed
carton of eggs,

cliques of chicks
all primped
bouncing
blue-and-gold hair bows
and Barbie-smooth legs,

lonely homelies
all pimpled
slouching
asparagus legs drowning in
their brothers' shorts.

But quickly quickly
  Skill
  Promise
  and
  Team Spirit

sliced through,

sniggering girly-girls
scrambled
with the rest of us
into a
glorious quiche
of mutual grins.

And as we clapped and whooped at the end,
some leftovers stood on the rim

but I am daring to be hopeful.

Trotting along the sidewalk,
salty and tacky with sweat,
I reek!

I reek with possibility.

Volleyball.

We won't find out results for a few days,
but right now,
bouncing through the neon blast of sunset,
I reek,
and
nothing can stop my grin.

Not even going home.

My Father,
Who Art Not in Heaven,
and never will be,
sometimes
doesn't come home
from work
until two a.m.

and for his own reasons
goes to my sister's room

before he goes
to his own bed.

I don't want to
hear
know
live here.

I am scared for her

but I am so glad
he doesn't

come to my room.

Yaicha is named after a song
by some group from the last century called the
  Pousette-Dart Band.

Something about a girl,
        a candle in the falling rain
        shining amidst the pain.
I kind of surprise myself
when I can picture Yaicha as that candle.

My father named Yaicha after the "haunting
  melody."

I wonder if he ever listened
to the lyrics.

I imagine living in
just the bathroom,
how I would make the bathtub my
bed at night,
a little Coleman stove to cook on,
toilet, running water,

wouldn't ever have to leave that room.

All my needs in
one
small
space.

Some kid
slams me into a locker
as he crashes through the crowd,
actually lays a hand on the side of my head
to get me
out of the way.

I lean against the locker a second,
fumble my French book,
trying to look like
I had intended to land there,

and this tall blond guy from the soccer team
Kyler
stops briefly with a light hand on my arm
to say,
"Okay?"

When I nod
he winks at me
and takes off,

but I seem glued to the cold metal door,
my flushed face turned
to follow his shoulders
weaving through the waning rush.

ImadeitImadeitImadeitImadeit
ImadetheTEAM!

I am airplaning to the school bus
laughing
    screaming
        choking
           whooping
   I don't care
ImadeitImadeitImadetheTEAM!

I burst into his basement
yelling about
making the team—
Jed smiles
in that quizzical way,
a question mark.

He could care less
about sports.

But he likes me anyway.

He pats the couch,
gestures to the TV.

"French Flame's on," he says.

I snuggle in
and Jed smiles
toward the beginning credits.

"Congrats," he says.

Rona is our setter
on the volleyball team,
quick-thinking and slippery,
a fuzzy-haired elf
with fingers that are
alien long.

She and her mom rent
a rickety calamity of a white clapboard house
on the west side.
She once said
I can't go over there
because
her dad is
sometimes sober,
but
sometimes he's not.

I think we could become really good friends.

All colors of the tortured rainbow
in succession,
black
blue
purple-red
yellow-green,

my hip bone,
Rona's swollen thumb,
someone's elbow,
someone else's calf
       where she kicked herself, for Pete's sake,
all body parts covered.

Learning to roll for a volleyball
gracefully
is painful business.

The ball drops
to the floor
between me and Carmen.
We stand silent,
          guilty glances.

Coach Roy cups his ear—
the team stutters,
"My-my ball-ball-ball!"

He leans harder with his ear
eyes wider
eyebrows dancing,

we all yell,
"MY BALL!"

He points a freckled finger
and grins—

Emma "MY BALL!"
Carmen "MY BALL!"
Doneesha "MY BALL!"

When he turns to me,

the heat I'm just discovering
screams,
"MY BALL!"

Hair on my arms
stands up
and about bursts into flame.

My lungs are claiming expanding territory.

This is my voice.

It is MY BALL.

Somehow
this is worse
than the normal yelling.

Quiet and earnest,
he is squatting in front of me.
I hunch on the couch.

"I know you think you want to play volleyball.
        —aren't I already?
Competition creates nastiness,
        —dissolves nastiness, you mean
a false sense of empowerment,
  an 'I'm better than you' euphoria—
        —my team is better than yours, maybe
  believe me, I know.
I wouldn't want you to get caught up in that,
the hunger for control over others.
When I was young blah blah blah blah . . ."
        —blah blah blah . . .

My hearing sinks into a cool, soundless cellar,

my eyes watch his thin lips moving against
   each other in silence,
and I know
that Darren and Yaicha were right
when they once used our father to teach me the
   meaning of the word
hypocrite.

When he finishes his oration with a
"Do we understand each other?"
I say,
"Yes, Father."

—*but you didn't specifically tell me to quit.*

Darren is named after a dead person.

When my parents were first married,

my father's best friend, Darren,
died in one of those unexplained car crashes
    where there's only one car involved and no
    bad weather, with the added mystery that
    the passenger was one of my father's female
    students.
She died, too.
Her name was Sarah,
but she didn't get anyone named after her.

"Will you *stop stepping* all over me?!"
Darren is yelling,
whipping the dish towel.
After dinner cleanup is getting dangerous.

I trip all the time,
I feel like
everyone
shares my body space.

From the kitchen corner
mom says
"She's growing, Darren,
give her some room."

"There *isn't* enough room
with her around.
She's like one of those
twenty-man saloon brawls
all by herself."
He slams a pot lid

into the cupboard.

I whisper,
"There ain't enough room
in this kitchen
for the both of us,
partner."

And mom shushes me
and says I'm not helping anything.

Sinking in my chair
staring at the carpet
as he coldly commands
that the waiter bring him
another steak,
the third one,
well
done
dammit
with
no
blood
inside,
the silence
ricocheting
from table
to table
to table,
appalled eyes
on my family.

Happy birthday,
Darren.

Rona has English before me.
"I aced it!" she exclaims,
slamming her tray next to mine at lunch.

"You usually do,"
I say,
meaning to be admiring—
        she's a great student—
but she looks hurt and slumps a little.

"You sure look tired,
it must've been hard," I try again.

Rona steals a salt-and-vinegar chip from
  my plate.
"I was up late studying."

Crunching, she amends that.
"No, I had finished studying in the afternoon,

but I was still up late.
Because my father was up late with
   his bottles."

Drinking.
My face crinkles in sympathy
         though I don't know what these bottles
            bring out in him.

"Till four thirty this morning," she adds.

Now I'm shocked.
"You didn't sleep till four thirty?"

"Almost five." She rubs her wrist across her
   nose and sniffs.

When she looks back into my eyes
her lashes seem wet,
but she's grinning.

"One hour of sleep, and I still aced it!"

I am scrunched in a corner of the cafeteria
   during study hall,
solving for x,
         where x is the number of paleontologists
            who can fit into a bus in Malawi when
            the ambient temperature is thirty-
            three centigrade.

      Whaaa?

Actually, I am
spying
on Jed.

I see him at home,
but almost never in school,
mainly because his senior classes are in the
   west wing.

He is talking quietly
at the far end of the room

with two friends, one short guy and one petite
blonde.
His car keys jangle,
they scoot out the side door,
and I feel the rumble of his Mustang.

We can't leave campus during the school day.

None of my business.

But funny to realize
he's a total stranger to me
in school.

I look at my calculations,
and it seems that x equals two paleontologists.

There must be something about
  Malawian buses
that I don't know.

In English class
Mr. Simon hands out pins,

QUESTION AUTHORITY

in brilliant yellow
to make us think, he says.

I wear it proudly all day
so people will
ask about it

but I
wouldn't
dare
wear it home.

Chewing gum
offends my father's
sensitive nature.

My mom used to
stash a small pack
for herself
in the uppermost
kitchen cabinet,
until once when I was little
I woke up at six a.m.
and snuck some to chew
for the half hour
before my father got up.

Swallowed it
to hide the evidence.

He made a big show of smelling my
breath,
dangerously, sweetly,
wanting to know where I got it.

I quaked in my jammies
but pointed to the cabinet.
It was the only time
he ever got really mad at
mom,
ranting on,
denting the fridge when he shoved a chair.
He called her
a cud-chewing cow,
he called her
stupid
for having gum where anyone could climb
from chair
to kitchen counter
to fridge top
to get to it.

And at age five I knew
that the tears he
brought to mom's eyes
he should have
brought to mine.

I am the only one named by my mother,
  whose name is Anne.

Anke means "little Anne" in Old German
but mom just loved the sounds,
        "Ahn—" like the gentle discovery of
        "—keh" a breath of changing weather.

I like her explanation better than just being a
diminutive
of somebody else.

Snippings, pieces, smiles

I pack end-of-summer photos in
my photo album

the one time we got mom in the canoe—

      leaving out the mean shots of
            Darren half drowning me,
            Yaicha smacking me with her
            paddle—

me and mom sitting with toes in the water,
me and mom cooking fish,

with captions, colored pencil, borders,

a grab at
a short history of me
in an impressive package.

I admire it

as I clean up the mess,
suffused with warmth of creation,

until Yaicha
walks in, and flips through
with derisive silence,

and at the end
says,
"There are only pictures of you and Mom!"

and I say to myself,
Exactly.

I grab
a package of six pairs,
and go find
Yaicha
gliding through
a sea of purses.

She fingers a popular thing
made from a shower curtain
        see-through
        with lavender and silver fish
a little smile plays on her mouth.

"They should line them,"
I say.
"You fill it with junk
and no one will
see
the fish."

Yaicha surfaces to glare
and sneer,

"Listen to the
Fashion Diva!"

pointing at the socks
in my hand.

But she purchases a purse
of flowery upholstery
instead.

Another Saturday of charity.

Angeline and I head for the kitchen
for a snack.

I open the fridge door
and poke—
yum, leftover pasta
        but that seems uncouth to offer her,
        somehow.

Angie lets out a small scream—
Yaicha is leaning
slim and silent on the back wall,
spooning up yogurt.
Yaicha's expression becomes devilish.
Uh-oh.
Scraping the bottom with her spoon,
  she warbles,
"Helloooo there, Angelllline."
She licks the back of her spoon

managing to make it a
threatening gesture.

"Um, hi, Yaicha," Angeline murmurs,
backing away one step.

My father slips in from the dining room.
"Ah, the angelic Angeline is with us."

"Oh, hello!" Angie says brightly, turning to him
in relief.

Yaicha's face slides back to sullen
as she edges sideways out of the room.

I watch her go,
wanting to follow.

In the chill evening
it builds until
he's raging at Yaicha,
and I freeze,
    the flannel cloth of my shirt
    blending me in with cabinetry.

Cyclone father
towers above her,
sucking papers off the counter,
hand raised with thunderbolts,
Yaicha crouching
on flowered linoleum,
beneath his
battering
unintelligible
roar,

and

shockingly

he's done

and walks out.

Debris swirls to the floor
around Yaicha,

and since there is nothing to say,
I put my limbs in motion,
walking woodenly
to my room.

When I was, like, five,
that redheaded girl down the street
used to ask
if she could come over.

We always played at her house.

Invite someone over?

No.

Nobody plays
at my house.

"Hey!"
Rona's yelling down the hallway,
her ponytail a copper fuzz bomb
bobbing on top of her head.

As we get closer
she says,

"The athletic slap,
not the girly whap!"

and we high-five with a cracking sound
that makes heads turn.

"Geometry." Rona holds up her book.

"Algebra." I grimace.

She shrugs, her lip to the side.
"All those word problems.
I think geometry's easier.
Doing proofs means you always know

when you're right or wrong."

Smacking my arm
she heads for class,
winking over her shoulder.
"Life should be that simple!"

Rona's humor is sometimes
         inappropriate.
She laughed out loud
when Jake's
custom chemo wig
blew off in the soccer crowd.
She got us
all giggling,
but Jake's red face
around a game grin
made me feel
kind of bad.

Rona snorted,
said
he probably needed
a good laugh—
counteract all that chemo.

Well, it *was* funny.

Our first game tonight,
at Plymouth High.

Their gym smells wrong.

I'm not nervous.
I'm not nervous.

No, really,
I'm not.

I'm a starting left-side hitter!

Jittered up, jacked up, amped up,
yes,
but
I'm not nervous.

The lights in here are pretty dim.

My god,

is that their team?
Look at that girl,
must be six-feet-something tall,
built like a jackhammer.

Okay.

I'm nervous.

We lost.

We couldn't pass the ball to save our lives,
and Plymouth just served us
to death.

Trooping onto the bus to go home,
we are all choosing
separate
seats.

Even Rona and I sit
apart,
each replaying
every bad pass, every hit into the net,
   every instance of not calling "mine."

My temple is against the rattling window,
eyes on the darkness
as we pull away from Plymouth High,

but all I see

is a white ball with blue stripes,

flying

out of reach.

"Who's depressed about Plymouth?"
Coach is standing over our leaden, silent team
while we stretch at practice.

Every hand goes up.

"What?" Coach Roy asks,
eyebrows dancing.

"I am," says Rona angrily.

I mutter the same right behind her.

"First game!" he exclaims.
"Learn from it.
But that game is over.
The rest of volleyball starts from here."

We are all looking up at him mid stretch,

our legs in Vs on the floor.

"Start fresh.
Remember we like this game!"

We smile a little,
glance at each other.

"Are you ready to play volleyball?" Coach Roy
  says.

Slowly, we stand up for our first passing drill.

"Yes."

"I can't hear you!"

"YES!"

I am not very big-breasted.

When I wanted
to get my first bra
        I was growing
        and they hurt
my father went berserk.

"Do they bounce when you
run across the street?"
        he roared,

        No, I said.

"Are men staring at them?"
        he roared,

        No, I said.

"Then you don't need a bra."

My mother didn't say a word

although she stood there
with me.

And the next day,
she bought me a training bra.

I was so proud.
I looked down at my breasts
snug in their new stiff bra
and thought,
Pretty soon they'll be so big
I won't be able to see my feet.

Well,
I stand by myself at the bus stop this morning,
looking down in experimentation
after more than a year of bras.

I can still see my feet.

Heavy hailstorm after lunch.
I ran outside and stood in it,
      spitting ice stinging my face,
      bitter nuggets on my tongue.

Coming back in,
gathering my language folder,
shaking out my hair,
Kyler watching me
from his locker down the hall
then turning to the back stairwell.

Squelching
sprinting
up the front stairs,
I screech to a kneel in front of class.

Retie my wet sneaker
four
slow
times,

hoping I am fast enough.

Kyler has Spanish
next door
when
I have French.

Madame DuPont
is pursing her fat lips,
tapping her watch
in the doorway.

If you don't like the weather,
wait five minutes.

Post practice
showered and clean
I step out to our backyard
lit by the sun's last rays,
my palm on the hemlock's trunk.

Ack—I'm smeared with sap,
　　　the bark oozing,
　　　　　　shouldn't trees be going dormant
　　　　　　　　soon?

Wipe sticky fingers on the dead lawn.
Now I'm tarred and feathered,
　　　furry with wilted grass
　　　and the bitty pinecones
　　　lying in a thick crunchy carpet beneath

the great tree.
My old climbing tree.

Aha!
I scoop cones into my sweatshirt pouch,
a bowlful the perfect centerpiece
for mom's fall stew.

As I step inside, cradling,
    —surprise—
    my father's home early.

He throws a glance at my loot,
says to mom,
"Tell her to take that crap back outside
where it belongs."

"I bought it with my own money."
Yaicha is backed into a corner
of the hallway,
held against the doorjamb
by our father's wrath.

"I will not have you tarting up your face
like a hooker!"
he thunders,
throwing her compact of blush
against a wall.

But look at her, I want to tell him.
She knows how to make it seem natural.

Yaicha scurries into her room.

He barrels through my shoulder as he
    stomps by,
and I am staring at

the tiny dent he made in the wall paint.

I pick up the plastic case,
slipping it into my back pocket
to give to her later.

It seems I move quietly in the darkened house
because
Yaicha doesn't hear me
come to the living room
as she sinks onto her heels by
   his favorite chair.

I watch her
open the compact
draw a fingertip across the makeup
and
luxuriantly
lovingly
smear a thick pink line low across the fabric of
   the chair back,
grinning at it wickedly.

I see Yaicha coming toward me in the school
  hallway
flanked by the two girls she's never without

and I get this funny little flutter inside,
and my hand leaps up—
"Yaicha!" I call out,
veering her way,
and she sidesteps me with a quick glare that
    glances off my temple
        and buries its blade
           in the wall
next to me.

Ah, all is good and normal with the world this
  morning.
What was I thinking,
greeting her out in the Social Open?

Kyler is ambling down the hall toward our
    algebra class
grinning at the antics of some louder
    soccer players,
in the conversation
but not being obnoxious.

At the doorway,
he lets the pack of them cram in before him,
politely gesturing,
still smiling.

I watch his tall frame disappear inside.

Suddenly
Rona is at my elbow.

"Whyoncha say something to him?"

Blushing furiously,

I wipe a hand over my hair.

Rona cocks an eyebrow.

I flip my palm up in exasperation.
"I don't know. . . ."
        What would I say?
"He's so . . .
nice."

Rona cackles and whacks my shoulder.

"Yeah, that's a real problem, all right."
And she leaves me
to walk into algebra
alone.

I pick at it
in algebra,
annoying little white thread,

and in the middle
of a square root
it lets go,

my shoulder exposed.

At the bell
Kyler pokes my skin—
"New style?"—
and grins.

I feel his touch
through lunch

raw,

charged.

Consider
picking out threads
on all my clothes,

the Fashionable
Open Seam
Look.

Struggling with uncooperative jeans
this morning,
thinking about yesterday when
Angeline said she saw that I
got selected for
Student Government Day,
one of twelve students—
she did, too.

She's terrified
of course
        how do we act?
        should we study?
like it's terribly important
or something.
                Not the blue shirt again.
                Is everything I own blue?
We're just
supposed to run
the town meeting,
visit the water-treatment plant,

pass some laws.

Should be a law against stains.

Is everything I own stained?

It's kind of an honor
to be chosen by all your teachers,
but Angeline's not
who I want
to hang out with
all day.

Hair in a ponytail? Down? Chop it off?

I find her so irritating,
predictable,
dull,

okay, *EVERY*thing is
irritating.

Not just Angeline.

I am supposed to be getting a ride home
  with him,
but walking down Main Street
my father greets this pretty woman friend,

and I force a loud sigh,
the only irritation
I can safely show,
knowing
it will be a while.

I stare at them,
arms crossed,
and up walks Angeline
in some frilly jacket.

"Hey," she breathes to me,
adoring eyes on my father,
who acts all excited
to see her,
runs a flat gentle hand

down her back.

Angie's expression is dripping
with sugar
as he turns back to his woman,
and
my next angry
exasperated sigh
farts out
at Angie.

"Oh, *please*,"
I mutter.

Hurt cow eyes
reproach me,
and Angeline sulks away.
Over her shoulder
I hear,
"Your dad is the greatest,
and you don't even
know."

As Darren came out
of the bathroom
this morning,
pulling shirt overhead,
the bruise
half his side
glared garish mauve

and I felt
my
        upholstery
                        rip
and bits of fluff
escape
to float away

before Darren
noticed me
and yanked
his shirt down.

And yet
when I was five
before bed
he would read to me
from *The House at Pooh Corner*
in all the voices—

> my favorite was Piglet
> the only time my father had a
> soft
> high
> tender voice

with Eeyore and Tigger and
all of Rabbit's friends and relations.

And I really think
you can't read to someone like that
without
a little teeny
bit
of
love.

Mirrors suck.

From the side,
half-inch plywood
topped with
brownish brown hair
taut in a ponytail
to give my blemished Roman nose the lead,
draped in a spaghetti-spotted tee,
men's Levis
to keep up with Freakish Leg-Lengthening
   Disorder,
wooden bead earrings from Yaicha's trash
         two years ago.

Quite a package.

My grandma used to say,
         "Nobody's going to buy you."

Well, that's apparent.

Not listening, but
hearing
way too much.

Banging
beyond the wall
rhythmic
numbing
hypnotizing
amplifying
      He's in there
hurting her
      He's in there
hurting her.

Hear Yaicha's
low
unending
moan.

Why am I not good enough?

At least he loves
Darren and Yaicha
in some way

even if it's horrible,
he shows them attention

and I am furniture
I get nothing
nothing
nothing
no
thing

or
at times I get
a knife-edge glimpse of

something scary.

I think that it is supposed to be good,
that I get less
from him

but I feel

worth

less.

PART
TWO

Little packet by Yaicha's bed

> I've seen them before—
> Marci takes the pill before school
> laughing in the girls' room,
> proof of her
> extracurricular
> activities

But I overheard Yaicha tell her friend
she's a virgin,

never even had a boyfriend,

so I don't get it.

And she storms in
snatches the packet
raging about privacy.

Bubbling panic
I go on the offensive—

"Why should *you* take the pill?"

My insides shred
as she glares a full minute

and I stand my ground
wanting her to tell me
tell me
anything,

but when I see pain
forming
on her retinas

I decide I don't want to know.

I run.

Hunched with his calculator
pencil whispers
scowling brow

formulaic incantations
bouncing knee

jutting vertebrae
like hackles
on a gravel pit dog.

Darren carves through
nightly calculus,
sculpting another perfect grade,

the ice cream I brought him
two hours ago
now
puddling milk.

Darren is down in his room.
Yaicha is cutting through the kitchen.
I am on the edge of the rocking chair by the
  couch.

Each of us
a corner
of an equilateral triangle

equidistant

corner angle spread as far
away
from the other two as possible
without breaking apart

but in that position
we can't get any closer.

Unless maybe we step together.

Government work again.
Standing inside the mauve front door,
waiting for Angie to come down.

Fake flowers.

Silk, I think they call them.
Hecho en Mexico
makes me doubt any worm wove them.

A little gift card
anchored under the vase.
IN HARD TIMES FRIENDS ARE THERE.

Plastic ribs on the backs of the leaves.
Stiff wire stamens inside the
rigid papery petals.
A vibrant lily-blue never seen in nature.
Lemon Pledge–scented.

Friends Are There?
What friend sends false,

when false needs to be dusted?
What friend sends false,
when reality
bends toward light
nods in a breeze
feels like butter
shimmers with amethyst
smells of jelly beans, tangerines,
    and pencil shavings
finally wilts and melts so you can throw it
    away and start with something new?

I pull out the fake lily,
shove it down
behind the entry table,
as Angie tromps downstairs.

Third-floor bathroom
first stall on the left,
I am squatting
over the stained toilet seat
reading the metal walls
and catch something fresh—

> Angeline
> Peachy-keen
> The boys would taste her
> But she's too green

If a glass of milk like Angeline
gets on a bathroom wall,
the scrawlers
must be running out
of ammo.

In the between-class crush
I feel a *fwap*
      sharp and quick
      on the small of my back
and whirl
to catch
the light wink,
the tilt of his mouth
before
Jed slides to a side hallway
and away.

I embrace my biology book,
cheered by
chance encounter.

Hit-and-runs.

Rona sets the ball
      I jump and hit the ball
      (hopefully over the net)
           sprint to the back wall
             tag the wall
run back to the net
where
Rona sets the ball
      I jump and hit the ball
      (hopefully over the net)
           sprint to the back wall
             tag the wall
run back to the net
where
Rona sets the ball
      I jump and hit the ball
      (hopefully over the net)
           sprint to the back wall
             tag the wall
run back to the net—

The drill is supposed to make you stronger
but
I am so tired
after eight sprints
I stumble like a drunk
and can't get off the ground.

"Next victim!" Coach yells.

"No thinking, ladies!
You are thinking too hard!"

Coach Roy is shaking his head
at me
after I take my approach,
jump with all my might,
and hit the ball hard
into the net
again.
The ball is supposed to go
over
the net.

I never realized
till now
how hard the brain has to work
to make the body do what it asks.

Or maybe how hard the body has to work
to ignore
the brain.

In psych class
      Ms. Taft
      had us draw trees

      one tree for the traits
      we get from our
      mother's side

      one tree for the traits
      we get from our
      father's side.

      My mom's side has
      many branches,
      caring, fair, physical appearance,
        passive, calm-headed under stress.

      My father's side has
      more branches,
      athletic, questioning, impatient,
        stubborn, tightwad,

opinionated, controlling,
quick to anger,
friendly to strangers

and I stare in terror
at his massive tree,
crisscrossing branches.

If all this tree is from mom
and all this tree is from him
where do I grow
my own branches?

In the middle of a nap
a thought snaps me awake
and I stare at Jed
a moment,
his eyelashes long and still.

He is the same age as
my brother
        —I never thought of this?
and for a few more
moments
I am weirded out,
like finding out your
        turkey sandwich is actually flamingo
            meat.
But I watch Jed
asleep,
and his familiar breathing
his hand on my hip
calm me
and I lay my face again
on his warm chest.

I love the hardware store
     cool circular blade
     hefty hammer
     greasy smell.

While my father gets what he needs,
I spend a long time
running my hands
through chain-link
     like chain mail
distraction
from thinking of

last time we were here

when we ran into Marci,

     the Marci with a big chest and blue eyes
     the Marci who's had most of the greatest
      guys

and I had to introduce her to my father.

As she left with her nails or screws or
   something,
I was standing near the front door—
she leaned in to my ear
and said, all breathy,
"Your dad is soooo handsome!"
with that oozy look in her eyes.

I watched her flick her hair and go,
leaving me gulping,
leaning on the rocking display rack of
   jackknives.

His Anger stands alone
stands erect
in the
middle of the room.

We step gently around it,
a terrifying totem pole
bristling beaks, pinions, talons.

I can't remember
when it started
when firm hand
        became
        fisted liege
                became
                feral
                        tyrannical
                                rage
                more important than
                the rest of us,
                but

it didn't used to be this way
and that
keeps us tied to him,
guessing,
teetering,
waiting,
while stepping around
his Anger
in the
middle of the room.

"And then my mother took me to Printemps,
   you know, that makeup superstore?
And I chose, like, four different shades of eye
   shadow?"
Angeline leans over the kitchen table,
eager to please me.

I am doing my best not to snore,
tilting on my chair's back legs.

Her short delicate fingers count off.
"Let's see, um, Café au Lait,
April Skies,
Twinkle Frost,
and Satin Sheets."

She blushes on that last one,
as my father moves smoothly into the room.

"Quite becoming on you," he drips
charmingly,

hand gliding over the back of her chair.

Angie's cheeks flood a deeper shade.

I gape at the man
gently placing his mug on the edge of the sink,
smiling his way out again.

Did he just compliment makeup?

I asked Angeline
about her father
only once.

She said
all airy,
"Oh, he'll leave that
floozy
and be back someday soon."

And I thought
>How old are you,
>that you believe
that crap?

I'm on my third burger,
Rona's on her fourth,
sprawled in BurgerMeister,
people-watching
after practice.

A horrendously large,
        I mean,
somewhat overweight
girl from school
gets the Double Dare with Extra Sauce
and Rona hisses,
"Look at those jowls!"

I slap her on the arm
in shock.

Her lettuce-draped mouth mumbles,
"Well, so she wants a burger.
She should at least exercise."

And before I can spit out anything

Rona yells,
"Hey, I hear the wrestling team's got an
    opening!"

When the poor girl turns to look,
her lips a chubby O,
Rona salutes her with a half-eaten burger
and a serious nod.

My pickle slice slips down unchewed.

Honesty takes a stomach
with one less burger.

The snarl of a motor
and a quick
bronnk of the horn,
Jed's blue-sleeved arm saluting me
as he roars past me through the school lot.

Must have had someone with him.

Didn't offer a ride,
but
at least I am wavable.

Relief,
a breather from Sunday Angie-sitting,
even if it's on my father's orders.

Stepping into my clogs,
waltzing slowly slowly out the back door,
swinging the full ash bucket,
shwwwsh
shwwwsh—

Whatzit called?
Centripi—something.

shwwwsh
SHWWWSH! Too far too slow some ash flies
   out running forward to escape,
        laughing at my own stupidity.

At the compost pile
dump the bucket,

"Cinderelly, Cinderelly!"
backing away as a small poof arises.

Twirl toward the house,
spinning with both hands on the handle,
empty bucket
flying in a captive circle.

One last crisp breath—
step back inside,
bucket clanging the door frame.

Kicking off clogs
in the stifling warmth
I see Angeline and my father leaning toward
   each other over the chessboard.

He's teaching her to play.

He's teaching Angeline to play something
only
he and Darren play.

Driving home from food shopping,
me in the front seat,
Yaicha in the back,
I am shocked when
my father slows to the side
for a slippery husk of a man
thumbing a ride.

Just before the guy
gets in
next to Yaicha,
my father says,
"But young girls should never do this.
Very dangerous."

Well, first of all,
I can't drive anyway,
and Yaicha's got her license
but who lets her use the car?

Second of all,
if the guy's an ax murderer

it's very dangerous for my father to
pick him up, too.

But he's driving smugly,
sparks of elation on his face,
enjoying the risk he's taken for us all.

Yaicha scrunches up against the car door
on her side,
legs crossed,
eyes on the pines going by.

The guy grunts
when he wants out
up the highway,

the smell of him
still hunched in the backseat
till we get home.

Mom's watering wandering Jews

and as I cut through the dining room
with my usual
        cheddar and crackers
the buffet table biffs me
in the hip—

I crumple,
cheese fumbles,

and without turning to me on the floor
mom mutters,
"Good Graces,
slow down.
That's an antique buffet."

The ancient leather
wingback chair
straddles boards on the porch.

I tuck myself
between the arms
        with Sleator, Asimov, Sones.

Then I see
tufts of stuffing
billowing from the hole in the seat

and something gray
running in panic
    —a mouse.

No,
not with that snakey naked tail.

I jump up,
my books drop.

They're rats.

Rona and I push off from my locker and head
   to practice.

Struggling with the strap on my gym bag,
I hear Rona say softly,

"Zat a bruise on Yaicha's chin today?"

My heart cramps up and can't do its job for
   one long beat.

"Yes" comes out in a hoarse whisper.
I give up on the strap,
letting it dig into my shoulder.

"Your dad?"

"Yes." How does she know that?

Rona starts swinging her duffel,
looking around nonchalantly

as we enter the gym.

"*You* never seem to have bruises."
And Rona would know,
we see each other changing clothing every day.

"He likes my sister and brother
better than he likes me."

Did I just say that out loud?

Rona asks questions all the time.

Things I don't really want to answer,
but I have to, somehow.

She's the only one I feel compelled to tell my
   reality to.

If I could just open my mouth wide enough
to allow those gagging blobs of truth
their slow, tar-seep passage
up through my gullet,
        with barely enough oxygen to keep from
           passing out
        while they glorp over my tongue,
those truths would reach my teeth,
        where if my jaw weren't unhinged,
I might bite them off
so I could
breathe again.

Sprained my right thumb
in last night's game
          —we pounded the Red Hawks—
so I proudly tape it up for school,
until some guys
jeer that I'm a pansy.

Which I'm not.
I mean, I can still play with a sprained thumb.

I rip off the tape
before French.

As I slip into my seat
Angeline points gently at
the darkening thumb
and whispers,
"Ouch. I mean, *ouille*!"

I shrug like I'm fine,

grant her
a quick grin

but at the boundary of
her sympathy
and
my irritation,
I take the grin
back again.

Dreaming of
rolling
rolling
rolling down
a warm grassy slope
laughing
rolling faster
rolling
rolling
into shadow
rolling
rolling
fear
rolling
cold
rolling
SMACK
into a tree.

I awake
on the living room floor,
moonless dark,

heart pounding,
my head leaning
against the leg of my father's chair.

Darren came into the kitchen
this morning,
black circles
around wavering eyes,
and he wouldn't look at any of us.

Mom said he was sick

but he's not sick.

I've seen this
a few times before

always after he and my father fight

and then

my father "talks" to him
in private

in his room
for hours

but most of the time
I don't hear their voices.

We are drinking Diet Coke
on the couch after dinner,
Mom and I.

She smoothes the black wool surface
with her wedding hand,
and says
before they splurged and bought this
furniture
when they got married,
my father
had an enormous broken armchair
they both squashed into,
and someone else's television box for
   a side table.
She says
they would read to each other
from a book of Ogden Nash,
my father stroking her hair.

I am floored.

Floored by her butter-soft eyes,

her caressing hand,
her fondness for the furniture
they bought together
in a time
of kindness.

I belong,
sweating team effort,
when the pass is right to Rona
when I run to her and spring
when my arm swing is on
when our timing is perfection
when I smack
        that ol' white leather butt
and the
opposing team scrambles,
stands erupt,
high fives all around,
singing together in the locker room.

    I ran track last spring,
    nervous
    every meet
            out there all alone
            against seven other girls
            on a narrow track.

    The strength felt good

but nothing
nothing
like this.

Only working together.
Only these girls.
Only volleyball.

YES! What a hit!
Oh no,
Oh no,
Oh shit, she's down.

What a glorious hit
great form
great grunt
hand on
ball down
straight down
      in her face,
      six-packed,
      floor-flat,
      disoriented,
      fighting tears,
      bloody nose,
I'm rushing in
offering aid—
      Can she feel it?
      Elation running slicing through me

through my hand
to her hand?

She only sits
on her haunches,
hand staunching
the river red
flowing south
to her mouth.

I grimace guilty apologies.

But *YES!*
A frickin' glorious hit!

After an hour of silence
in the library
studying
fake oak grain on cubicle walls,

I love the way my voice sounds
      startling
      strong
      confident
as I give a woman in teetering heels
directions
to the school office.

We just happen to be walking to
  the east wing
at the same time.

Finally Angeline says,
"You're tall, you've really gotten tall."

I hmph.
I mean, duh.

Now she's walking sideways to face me,
earnestly explaining herself.

"No, really! You've grown so much lately!
It's so incredible!"

I stop in the middle of the hall
fist on my hip—

"Believe me, Ange,

I am aware that I have grown!"

I set my size-ten feet in motion as she reels in
   her shock
and scampers after me.

"But, really, tall looks good on you.
You're going to be beautiful!"

I peel off at psych class as she continues to
   world history.

Angie was digging a hole for herself,
but I find myself
wanting to
believe
the last thing she said.

I can see from my bedroom window
that his Mustang is not parked under the
   oak tree.

Where is Jed?

We haven't had our nap in days.

Possessed for three seconds.

Some demon jumped
into my mouth
flapping my tongue with its claws
to say
words I'd never thought of—

"Yaicha, I was talking
to *mom*.
You don't give a shit
about my life, so
why don't you just *shut up*?"

—and my jaw drops down
and Yaicha's
and Mom's.

And then the demon is gone,
so I can mumble
"sorry"

to my sister.

And I stand here
in dumb
confusion
while they continue conversation.

Where the hell
did that come from?

My father pokes me
nastily
in the side.

"You'll probably
never
get the nice rounded
curves of
a full woman.

You've always
been skinny,
always will."

I can feel
each
reclusive
bone
poke through,

the bones of
Embarrassment,

Anger,
Relief.

I push some back in,
but leave
Anger
sticking out.

Walls are thin.

Doesn't matter
what they are made of—
wood and plaster
wood and plaster and concrete block
wood and plaster and concrete block and
     corky soundproof panels
      like in the music room at school.

Doesn't even matter
which wall the bed is against,

I can hear
everything.

I mean,
WHY can't she just tell on him?
It's just words.

Just
open her mouth
and out come those words.

And then he'd be stopped.

Right?

I stare hard at Yaicha
during breakfast.

She's good with makeup
really good
from being in plays and musicals.

I stare at the smudge,
purpling black
on her jaw,
barely buried under makeup.

Okay.
She isn't
good at it
just because of plays.

It's cold enough this morning
to want to stand
in front of the woodstove
after stoking it for the day.

"Hey, quit
soaking up
all the heat!"

Darren and I
say that every time
and shove each other
in jest,
and every time
Mom says we deserve each other.

It's one of about
only three
things I know how
to do
with my
brother.

Jed's peeling out
in the school parking lot.
Why doesn't it
make me laugh,
        twirl,
    shout!
like
Ginger and Marci?

I stand alone
crossing my arms
eyes rolling
making that
        "you are such an idiot"
        sound with my tongue.

When Jed has left just a cloud,
Ginger and Marci
glance at me,
then pointedly roll eyes at each other.

Something as dumb as

burning rubber
rattles
my cardboard box of structure.

This is why
I am not popular,
I think.

Untwisting my bra strap
in the middle of the hallway

and there is Jed coming out of room 32
in serious discussion with another guy.

I blush his way,
feel a little thrilled at showing off my bra strap
  in front of him

but his eyes glide over my head
as he answers a question,
missing me entirely.

I got an A on the third quiz in
  American history,
an A,
dammit.

Last time I got a B

up from a C

and my father said,

"If you can get a C
you can get a B,

If you can get a B
you can get an A."

So I got an A in American history,

which I only studied hard in
because Mr. Parks is more like
  a friend to everyone

than a teacher
and we got to interview this
  hundred-year-old man
who's lived here
forever
and remembers when Cartwright Street
was only a horse trail
and the mill at Mill Pond
actually worked.

I got an A
and my father said,

"Grades don't mean anything."

He was reading in his chair
I was reading on the couch
both of us reading
and drinking hot tea
in the evening
just like a peaceful father and daughter.

I bumped my cup
and scalding tea sailed
all into my jeans
burning hot
burning me
and he slammed his book down
yelling,

"You are so stupid!

What a stupid thing to do!"

Like I did it on purpose
to spoil his night

Like I wasn't in enough pain

And I started to cry
running away to rip off my jeans
ice my leg
ice it
ice it.

When I washed my angry face
and came back
he was reading in his chair
ignoring

the puddle of tea
the fallen cup
still wallowing on the couch.

I am
dumb
as wood,
old
dry
brown
hardened
splintering
flammable
unfeeling
resistant
jammed
un
speak
ing

table
bench
chair

footstool.

Long ago
we stood in the kitchen,
my mother
my father
and I,
hugging in a cluster
when my father
came home from work.

From their knees
I leaned way back to see
warm soft gazes for each other's faces,
and the velvety kiss,
until I pulled their attention
to me
down low.

They laughed,
tousled my hair,
and
we all said
I love you.

Knee pads at my ankles,
covered in the brine of practice,
I tromp into the kitchen
and he's there.

Shit.

Why is he home so early?

My father downs what seems like an entire
   quart of water
in one long swallow,
staring around his tall glass at my damp
   person.

He carefully places the empty tumbler on the
   counter,
turns precisely on one foot,
leaves the kitchen

without a word.

So.

Before,
he didn't want me to play
and there was almost a conversation going.

Now he for sure knows I am still playing.

Why doesn't he say anything?

Yanking jeans over sweaty postpractice skin,
knowing taking a shower would amplify
where I've been.

I come out of my room,
Darren comes up the stairs,
and our father comes from the bathroom,
        a damp bath towel dangling
        from forefinger and thumb.

"Whose," he intones at me in the hallway,
    "is this?"

Darren holds out his hand.
"Mine," he whispers.

Our father looks surprised.
Did he think it was mine?

He breathes in,

launches the offensive at Darren.

"HOW MANY TIMES HAVE I TOLD YOU TO
  HANG THIS . . ."

louder and louder

words crushing together

in a piling roar

except in excerpts

"YOU THINK YOU CAN JUST DO WHAT YOU
  WANT . . ."

"I AM THE ONE WHO KNOWS WHAT'S GOOD
  FOR YOU . . ."

and suddenly I realize

he's actually yelling at me

      about volleyball.

I want to make him turn to me

yell at *me*

I want to yell at *him*

      I am here

      right here

I am not furniture—

But when his hand
smothers Darren's face with the wet towel,
shoving him hard into the wall,

I am backing away.

Darren is tromping upstairs
in work boots
and a black scowl,

heading out back to split wood

and as he cuts through the living room
swerves toward our father's chair

gives the leg a vicious kick
so the chair rocks up on two legs
and
bangs down again,

Darren already jerking open the back door
to a blast of fresher air.

Indian summer
crowding
at the farmer's market,
Mom's requested squash in a string bag
scraping the goosebumpled skin
  below my shorts.

I crush
lemongrass
with my thumbnail,

breathing
sharp cleansing.

Mr. Ogawa
nods,
gestures with a bok choy
toward my calves.

"Leg like deer!"
bobbing

grinning
his compliment.

I flush pride at my volleyball strength,
bob my head, too.
What a sweet gentle man.

The best smell in the whole world
is
hot
popcorn
      slathered in decadent
      criminal amounts
      of butter
cooked in the old copper-bottomed pot.

Lights off.

I bury my face in my bowl,
the three of us kids
      watching
      Some Like It Hot with that
       hysterical Jack Lemmon,

munching together

parallel gazes.

Man, I'm Starvin' Marvin
running to meet Rona,
there she is,
close to the front near the salad bar
but
oh,
Angeline just behind her.

I stop mid hurry
        a girl slams me from behind,
        we murmur sorry
but all sound dims as I watch unnoticed,
        my best friend
        and
        my constant twitch

        the daring
        and
        the whimpering

        the architect
        and

the timber rot

the solid earth
and
the space walk, holding your breath
   because you forgot your helmet.

Maybe they said hello
when they first got in line.
Now they simply ignore each other,
inches apart with their trays.

We don't need to be a threesome.

I sidle into the ragged tail of the lunch line.

"So who the hell cares?"
Rona throws three carrots down with minimal
   crunching.
"Not like she's a friend
or an enemy, right?
She's nobody.
So why does Angeline bug you?"
She whips those blue eyes my way,
and all I can do
is swallow my hummus
and shrug.

A thought forms—
I shove it down.

Something about
my father.

Errands on the way home.
My father jogs across pavement to his office,
I stay in the parking lot
watching sparrows' rusty
heads
pop-in-pop-out
of car grills

nibbling bugs
spitting out papery wings
wiping grubby beaks.

On each car
a tiny
bird-sized neon sign:
DINNER BUFFET!
SMORGASBORD!
EAT AT JOE'S GRILL!

My father reappears,
hugging some blonde
half his age good-bye

kissing her fully longer,
sexier
than a married man
should even imagine.

He walks to our car,
smug.
I turn back to the birds,
glance at their
happy meal
and feel
a familiar familial nausea.

Homework.
Efficiency models
for the environmental psych unit.

What I Can Live Without

cars
cell phones
wall-to-wall carpet
furniture
whitening toothpaste
grape soda
Polo cologne
growing at the speed of giant kelp
that glue smell from the woodworking shop
Ginger's snorky giggling
Madame DuPont's fish-pale eyes
Angeline's whiny voice
choosing sides
a father

There's Jed
strolling up his driveway
with a senior buddy
in the indigo evening.

He wasn't home
all afternoon
and I am
suddenly
furious and garter-snake-striped with jealousy.

I want to run out there,
plant a real estate
SOLD
sign
between this guy
and Jed.

That's it.
I'm officially nuts.

Both hands in
Yaicha's wastebasket,
digging
while she's down
in the laundry room.

Crinkly Snickers wrapper
plastic promo case
sleek Clinique compact
        corners still packed with Sugar Toast
stained satin ribbon
Fashionista receipt
fermenting apple core

I stop at the racy lacy bra
        —no way did mom buy that—
worn to weariness,
elasticless.

I usually don't find much
but

search under pressure,
my heart-pounding glimpse
of
Yaicha's world.

"Let's go camping tonight,"
I say softly
to Yaicha,
starting the game
     where I reach out
     and she does what she wants
     with it.

Her eyes pointy and dark
she throws words out of her mouth.
"I hate camping."

Staring back
I whisper
"I hate this *house*."

"You don't know anything.
He'll never let us go."
She thunks the back of her head

against the kitchen wall.

"He'd never let *you* go.
He'd never notice
if I was gone."
I try a small smile,
nudge her,
"He's got a meeting.
Mom'll let us go.
I'll get the tent."
I hold my breath.

Thunk
with her head,
she turns away.
"I hate camping."

Game over.

In the attic
watching my exhales fog and dissipate
over a stage of life,
a cast of
cast-off
furniture and relics,
a dull palette of gray
in the worn-out gloom.

The ancient pine banana box
filled with Grandma's tea pieces,

the huge empty rococo frame
        garish even in dust,

the oak stool, folding table, sagging armchair
        from Aunt Sepha's house,

all unnecessary,
superfluous,
not worthy of life downstairs,

hidden away
like unused emotions

chilled to a crisp.

Unhappily comfortable here,
cold tears course
trails over my cheeks
like Olympic skiers,
crashing over the precipice of my jaw
in a spectacular
agony of defeat.

Yesterday afternoon
my father and I
tiled the bathroom floor
while everyone was out.

No praise.
No critique.
No words.
No one there worth talking to.

His section of tile was perfect.
My section of tile was perfect.

He didn't show off our work
when everyone got home.

I showed mom which section
was mine,
but I don't think she believed me.

After dinner
I chiseled a chip

out of one of his tiles
next to
the toilet.

Transparency girl.

Darren even sat in my chair for his breakfast,
my glass of OJ right there in front of him
waiting for me.

Walking to school
instead of waiting for the bus
because I am
so
damn
grumpy
this morning,

hoping
the smell of autumn
will revive me.

"Red-and-yellow,
gold-and-brown,
autumn-leaves-are-falling-down,"
in time with my feet,

knowing it sounds juvenile,
even saying it
out loud
convincing, convincing,

but pretty soon
it's just a jumble of
consonants,

a rhythm
for my
brain to pound by.

I have stopped for a mocha at Johansen Java,
lower lip on smooth plastic lid,
listening to Tight Yoga Suit explain to
  Over-Dyed Poodle Perm how starting up
    a gallery for her son's artwork is not a
    selfish act,
smelling warm raisins as the elderly man next
  to me breaks open a steaming scone,
     mumbling that he's fine, he's fine,
     he'll stay in his house no matter what
      that goodfernothin' son says,
patting some little boy with bedhead as he
  chokes on crumbs,
    his tattooed mother yapping into her
    phone about the water bill,

and I feel a fuzzy warmness toward humans.

Disparate,
fascinating,

bonding with a cup of joe in the same place.

Eavesdropping on strangers
gives more insight into a life
than having a conversation with someone you
  know.

People are more honest
when they don't know you are listening.

"I don't know, she just—
she just doesn't interest me."

Kyler is sitting behind me in algebra,
answering a grilling by his friend.

"Fake nails,
all that white skin,
doesn't she go outside?
A person should go outside sometimes,
feel the weather."

His pencil eraser is bouncing
tok
tok
tok
on the desktop.

"I mean, yeah, she's hot,
but . . ."

The teacher clears her throat and Kyler goes
  quiet.

I like the "but."

Rona and I
each in our own bus seat
lie on our backs
feet out the open windows
as we head back home.

We just barely won
against Raeburn
and we didn't "play up to our potential"
but hey
another win.
Our 8-2 record has us heading for the state
   tournament.

Rona and I
hang our heads off our seats
into the aisle,
watching a Barbie player
put makeup on her sweaty face,
and roll our eyes at each other.

Probably forgot to bring deodorant

but her face
will be all dolled up.

Smoothing on lipstick,
Barbie catches my eye and shrugs,
and we grin at each other.

To see her primp
you'd never know how tough she is on the
    court.

One of the toughest.

Sweaty in my sweats,
I step into the kitchen.

"Where'd you come from?"
Darren asks,
dish towel dangling.

Yaicha butts in,
all business at the sink,
"She's playing volleyball."

Darren's eyebrows fly up.
"Yeah? Cool,"
and
with a fierce scowl
he snaps the towel
at me.
I dance away
suddenly agile
and he flicks the table leg
instead of mine.

Snuck out to a party
at the Forsters' half-framed house—
snuck,
      yeah,
            like anyone at home noticed I left.

Tired of meandering
between
knots of dull conversation,
I hunker down onto the unfinished porch steps
mittens around my two-hour beer,
listening to Kyler explain to someone
where the back trailhead is for Mount Logan.

"No, that's the main trailhead you're
  thinking of."
Kyler is itching his head
      through his hand-knit hat.

Before I can think, I say,
"The back trailhead starts off the highway,

near the twelve-mile marker."

Kyler turns,
earflaps swinging.
"You've done that hike?"
He lets out a whistle,
reaches over to push my thigh with a gloved
    hand.
"All the way to the top?
You're strong, volleyball girl!"

"Good oxygen up there in July," I say,
grinning madly at his compliment.
"And we had a black-mama-bear encounter
    halfway up."

The other guy snorts,
"Bet you ran with your tail between your legs."

Kyler's warm brown eyes examine mine.
"No, she didn't," he says.

"You don't run from black bears,"
    I say to the guy,
but I'm gazing at Kyler,
heart thumping.

No one is home.

I stand poised
midroom,
woofers buzzing the windows.

And when
shrieking guitar strings
rip me free
I begin with the desk chair,
throw it to the side,
spin the desk
        to the center
                of the room,
shove the bed
        momentarily in front of the bedroom
         door
        then against the far wall,
plow the desk smack against baseboards,
ram the chair home,
crash the dresser in the corner,
flop the carpet open to the left,

whirl
with fingers wide,
the beat fades,

and
I stand poised,
arm hair on end,
in a new country.

Startled out of a light nap,
my face against the couch back.

Jed wraps an arm around my shoulders
to roll both of us
so he can reach the ringing phone.

I consider grumbling.

"Yuh. Yuh. No, nothing important,
just napping."
He yawns.
"Sure, let's go now. Yuh. See ya."

He tosses the phone to the other end
   of the couch,
tapping my back three times,
Jed language for "I need you to move."

I shift,

squinching my eyes like I had been sleeping.

He eases out from under me and stands,
"I gotta go,"
stretching long arms,
another long yawn with canines showing,
and he tosses his coat over his shoulder.

"See you tomorrow, I guess," and he's loping
    out the door,
leaving me sprawled,
unnapping,
alone in his basement.

I glare at the texture of the ceiling,
trying not to cry.

Last night
a group of us from volleyball and some guys
saw that movie
about all the world's nuclear power plants
   gone wacko
and the guy next to me
actually took my hand
early on
and didn't give it back.
We held hands through most of the movie
for some reason.
When the reactors melted down in
   enormous explosions
he gripped my fingers so hard
my rings bit me
and I pulled back.
He let go and kind of stretched.
I was able to enjoy
the rest of the nuclear meltdown with
   feeling in my fingers,
but I felt

like I was the only one in the theater.

And at the end of the movie
the boy-romantic-interest lived,
of course.
The girl-romantic-interest passed out from
  radiation exposure
and it was clear
she'd never make it.

Lying on my side
in my old running tights
on the black couch,
        elbow cocked
        head propped
reading, my usual
escape.

My father walks in,
stops in the middle
of the carpet,
contemplating me.

"You are getting to be
very sexy," he says
quietly
in a reverent tone
I don't like at all.

I sit up fast
snap shut my book
fist clenched

mouth dry
controlled walk past him
down the hall
to my room
close the door
back away
back away
breathe.

Don't look at me.
Don't look at me

ever

again.

The boys' soccer team swaggers by our
   pregame warm-up.

"Whoa!
Did you see—
that girl can *hit*!"

The team clown is performing loudly for us.

"What's her name?
What?
Anke?"

Kyler jostles him
to keep him moving,
and throws a wave and a smile to me.

The guy is still at it as they amble out
   to the fields,
"I want her on my team!
Hey, Anke!
Wanna be on my team?"

I am blushing
as I run back to the end of the hitting line,
blushing
but grinning.

Guys sure are obnoxious.

Swapping
ProBars after our big win,
      half my peanut butter
      for
      half Rona's chocolate malt.
We chuck the crumpled wrappers to each other
grunting,
super slo-mo,
grunting
like we're hitting the volleyball.

I holler
"MINE!"
as her wrapper flies to me,
and toss it back
over her head
"Go, Rona, *GO!*"
screaming at her
as she
dives to the grass

and rolls to a stop at the foot of the tree.
"YEAH, RONA!"

Her on the ground holding up the wrapper,
me with my hands up in victory,
"The CROWD GOES WIIIILLLD!"
Two senior guys stroll by,
      eyebrows raised.
We grin.

Volleyball has taught me to yell.

Yawning at my locker,
gathering English books,
when a long body grazes my back and
   there is Kyler,
looking a little breathless.

"Hey, caught you," he says, flashing a grin.

"Hey, Kyler!"
Was that too enthusiastic?
And I love that green shirt on you.

He rubs a hand down his sleeve.
"I was wondering if you were going to the
   Harvest Dance."

Okay, panic.

"I, um, yeah, I'm going.
Probably with Rona, you know,
not as a date, ha! but, well,

I don't think I should go and just dance with
   one person all night,
you know?
So I was going to go with friends
and just dance with whoever I want."

Way too much talking.

But Kyler is nodding,
"Yeah, that's what a bunch of us are doing,
   as well.
But I was hoping you'd save me a dance?
Or two."
Squeezes my forearm and laughs a little.

"Sure! Thanks!" I squeak.
Dammit—I hate squeaking.

"Great!" he says,
sliding his hand off my arm
in a trail of warmth,

"Gotta get to chemistry."

He walks down the hall backward
hands gesturing rising bubbles
with a pop-pop-pop of his lips,
then he waves
and turns the corner.

Changing into
my uniform,
ignoring all the locker-room babble,
thinking of Kyler,
wondering
why he seems to like me.

Thrilled he might like me!

But I don't get it
and
I don't really believe it
because
there are so many cute girls
and I am basically
a nothing freshman with big feet and a newly
   discovered pimple on the side of her nose.

On the bus
to an away game with Robins-Hancock,
zoning to tunes,
teammates around me
bouncing in their seats.

My mind travels to
this family of crows
in the woods next door,
cackling, chuckling, creating ruckuses and
   general wild rumpuses,
each one
involved with the next one,
knowing who likes to sit next to who among
   the pine needles,
shuffling in a file on the limb
so everyone is finally comfy.

I smile, watching,
as they ruffle and rattle their feathers,

all their emotions
laid out on the branch,
      so to speak,
no secrets,
no wondering what the crow beside you
  is feeling.

Kind of like my volleyball family.
Just as noisy.
Fewer feathers.

Rona drops me off
into windy darkness at the bottom
  of the driveway,
a shuffle of leaves
blown against my feet,
and I stand still,
listening.

Acorns plopping onto damp asphalt,
moaning of hemlocks,
a high whine of air
        whisking around the corner
          of the house.

It's stirring energy out here.

A yellow angle of light from the kitchen
scrapes the back lawn.

My ponytail whips my face
with the first smattering of drops,

so I head in
before the deluge,

though I'd rather stand out here
to hear rain pelting the oak trees,
than go inside
and hear what's there.

Yaicha is crying gently
in the bathroom.
Darren,
hesitant,
goes in.

What I hear,
        flat against the hall wallpaper,
is the lift at the end
of Darren's soft sentence,
        a question.

And Yaicha's voice
flat as mud at low tide,

        "I'll live for now.

        You know
        he said he'd kill me
        if I told.

        He'd kill me."

And I hear it,

            a wooden mast snapping
            from years of termites below—

I hear it
and know

it is true.

He would kill her.

Can't sleep through it
so I pad to the kitchen.

Earphones on
huddling on the stool
cuddling hot chocolate.

In she comes,
glazed
and frayed,

leans on the
butcher block
then lays her cheek
on the smooth
scored
wood.

I am still
as brick
and then crack,

click off my music,

push my steaming cocoa
across the maple
to Yaicha.

Her fingers wrap
the scalding mug,

eyes closed.

. . . and i'm jealous!
with a sick
acidic
burbling
bile
i want what they have

as horrible
curdling
vile
as it is
darren and yaicha
get more
than
me.

Sometimes
first thing in the morning
when I walk down the hallway before class
shouts and hurrying footsteps and laughter
   spin off,
sucked away by a whirlpool,

and I could be alone,
deaf,
a different sort of fish
in this vast school of shining matching silver.

And it takes something physical—
        the vice principal's hand on my arm,
        "You all right, Anke?"
to bring me back.

Walking home alone,
cooling sweat.
An odd afternoon of fog
slaps softly like a damp paper towel.

My breath feels thick,
striding past the soggy soccer field,
around the goal post
off the edge of the grass.

Entering birch trees,
a dove careens by,
mockingbirds holler,
wind washes the carpet of yellow leaves.
Rounding the path's curve
a slice of fall glances my jaw
and my nose opens
to take in something sharp,
something easier to breathe,
an acrid, lively, nervous smell
that says something cutting and different
is on its way.

He went into Yaicha's room
last night
after he hit her
across the mouth
for reading
Cosmo magazine.

I burned in my blood,
I turned to Mom
as we stood in the hall
and inside my head screamed,
　　　DO something!

Her eyes glazed and wide
like an injured cat,
her mouth pulled tight,
Mom sighed in a voice that didn't match,

"It'll be okay.
He's just making peace with her."

And she walked away.

It just occurred to me.

It's her choice.
Yaicha chooses not to tell anyone
and Darren does too

and Mom.

Am I the only one bothered by this?
I mean
bothered enough to think about it?

So all the pressure is on me,
the Youngest and Most Bothered.
Or maybe I am just
outside enough,
being the footstool observing from the corner,
that I have a view of reality.

And I can't stand it anymore.

Why me?
I don't need this crap.

Then
why don't I tell on him?

If they don't,
why don't I?

Because.

Because I am safe this way,
silent
unnoticed.

Because my family would crack
snap
shatter
      like pine boughs in an ice storm
jagged pieces scattered,
irreparable,

and there would be no family

and I don't want that on my head.

What we have is better than that.

Right?

Squid ink black dreaming,
Running hard,
running from,
from my father
in that mask,
running to,
to the school
bell's ringing
incessant ringing,
late late late,
volleyballs
rolling in the hall,
Angeline
Angeline
pestering
pestering,
pushing by people
to get to me,
I am panting
with exertion
backed up against it,
Jed slouching

against my locker,
pointing at me,
no expression,
pointing,
I wear no clothes,
the entire
student
body
halts
to stare in silence—

bursting to breathe,
I look down to find
I have
a penis.

PART
THREE

I should have worn polypro liners
inside my work gloves this morning.

Brittle frost,
and I am lugging dead branches from
   the front yard
into the side woods.

Usually I just haul ass and get it done,
keeps me warm.

Today I am shivering in my plaid flannel shirt,
staring into the windows of our house,
my perspective skewed
to an outsider's.

Why am I suddenly uncomfortable?

Up till now
life was just normal.
Maybe not normal for everyone,

but *my* normal.

I used to feel solid,
knowing my job in this house—
      silence, blinders, stillness.

Now
I feel like a lumberjack
with a nail file instead of an ax,
out of context,
frustrated,
looking around me to kill time.
Except that I am noticing things.
And being bothered by them.

I don't like it.

I don't want to think about it.

"Hey," I say, shifting my backpack,
standing in his basement doorway.
"No practice today, lighting repairs."

Jed pats the couch,
eyes on the television.
"Have a seat," he says absently.

Wow.

What an invitation.

"Um, no thanks.
I have algebra problems to finish."

I have never made an excuse before.

"Oh. 'Kay, do a good job."
He smiles,
but his eyes swing back to the TV,

and I am so out of here.

I've been telling Rona all about Kyler,
having talked to him, like, what, twice?

Peeling a pale slice of tomato off her sandwich,
she slaps it onto her tray.
"So why is he in chem class as a freshman?"

Trust Rona to point out I don't know him at all.
"Must've tested out of bio?"

Rona whacks her sandwich back together,
chomping through the middle with gusto.
"Musht be shmart," she mumbles.

I nod,
blowing steam off my chili.
"He was nervous, even asking me for a dance."
I dump the spoonful back in,
feeling disappointed.
Aren't guys superhuman about their feelings?

"Well, no shit, Anke,

you're this tall, gorgeous, amazing
   volleyball player,
even if you are a freshman."

I roll my eyes.

She waves her milk,
spraying liquid from the straw.
"You are, even if you're too blind to see it.
And he's smart, not asking you for a
   big commitment,
just a dance or two.
But if you'd said no, how devastating would
   that be to a good-looking guy?
I mean, not that he's really popular or
   anything,
and neither are you—"

"Gee, thanks for reminding me."

"—but he's supposed to be a great
   soccer player,

and his buddies would sure give him shit if you
  refused to dance with him."

Like I *would* refuse to dance with him.
Flexing the styro bowl,
it finally cracks.
"Wanna go to this Thursday's soccer game
  with me, Rona?"

Under lights on Thursday night,
end of the second half,
tied with Westland 3 to 3,
shouts of fans crystallizing midair
at the coldest soccer game on record.

Rona shrieks through her scarf,
razzing the ref.
I am hopping for circulation,
clapping mittens,
      thinking how smart I am,
      wearing tights under my jeans.

Kyler is back in the game with less than a
   minute to go,
right wing,
he has the ball,
a fluid body speeding downfield.
Westland is on us,
but Kyler does this special spin,
taking control again,

his defender lurching—
       without thinking I belt out,
         "GO, KYLER, GO!"
       up on my toes—
and suddenly he feints left,
passes to our center,
who passes back,
Kyler taps it once,
then kicks the ball past the goalie's glove into
   the high left corner of the net in the last five
   seconds and we've won the game!

"Yeaaaah!"
I grab Rona's shoulders,
bouncing together
in a screaming mass of elated faces.

As players flow to the side
Kyler catches sight of me,
       his eyes light up in recognition,
       the widest smile ever.
Pulling off a mitten to give a thumbs-up

I grin back
and he's carried on with the
    crowd's enthusiasm,

but he smiled right at me,
me,
personally.

Oh my god
that's Darren
leaning against the stage
at the far end of the court.

I've never seen him in the gym.
Ever.

His arms are folded over a textbook,
and he's doing his
breathing through his nose thing
like he's checking the atmosphere for foreign
    substances in parts per million,
no expression I can see from here.

We finish our drill
and I manage not to shank the ball
    into the bleachers
in front of my brother.

Now we go over hitting coverage
and I feel a bubble of elation

for some reason
as Darren watches us.

He stands there the whole drill.

I pretend to suddenly see him,
raise a casual from-the-hip wave.
His small smile flashes
and he pushes off the stage
to head to debate club.

I lean to the girl next to me.

"That's my brother, Darren."

After volleyball practice
I spot Jed walking parallel to me across the lot,
and he angles over.

"Want to walk home today? It's pretty warm,"
  he says,
throwing an arm over my shoulders.

It's been days since he's even said hello.
"Careful," I say, grimacing,
"you're touching a freshman in public."

That crooked lip sets my heart dancing,
dammit.

"So? Senior guys can get away with it.
It's the young girls who get the reputation."

I pull out from under,
pissed.
"That's exactly it,"

and I walk three steps out to the side of him,
arms folded.

Jed pulls at my arm,
laughing,
trying to uncross me.
"C'mon, Ank, you of all people don't have a rep."

Wondering
if that's good or bad,
I let him release one tucked arm.

"Aaaah, I need a nap," he says in a yawn,
squeezing my forearm and letting it go.

Does he ever do anything else?
"Hey," I say, bopping his bicep,
"let's walk home through College Woods!
　　　Take off our sneaks, put our toes in the
　　　　icy brook."

His right eyebrow goes up.

"In October?"

Not his thing.

But napping is.

I wish I'd taken the late bus home.
Jed can't possibly be this worn-out after
two or three of my kisses,
I'm not that good.

But he's snoring.

Do I need a nap?
No.

Do I need kissing?
Definitely.

There has been an imbalance
   between the two lately.

And maybe there's another guy out there
who might enjoy
kissing me more.

When I come into the dining room,
French book in hand,
Yaicha doesn't even register me.

All these cool charcoal rubbings
cover the table
and she hovers on tiptoe
darting in
moving one pattern close to another
tipping back for a different perspective
moving a piece minutely
knocking her rings on the table
  as she contemplates.

I glide into view.
She shuffles through wall textures
heating grates
fig leaf veins
sneaker soles

and shifts focus toward my face.
 I gape when I see the bright bruise

under her left eye.

Un-make-upped.

She glares defiance,
says nothing.

It's not really that Yaicha sat before everyone
  else at the table.

This time it made him angry.
Next time it might not.

I know it's not Yaicha.
Or Darren.
Or me.
Or mom.

It's him.

Inflict.
Dominate.
Impair.

It's all him.

Psycho-man.

And live-in victims

assuage him,
keep him hidden
from
the rest of the world.

I suppose in that way we are useful.

"Your father must have
info like that."
Angeline is at me
again.

Mom is making me work with her
on topics for government
and Angie is
forever formulating festering questions
to present
to Authorities,
Officials,
and suspicious
Politicals.

"He must have
books and books,"
Angie is pleading.
"He's a professor."

I'm not asking
him

for anything.

I want to say,
> *Get over your goddamn crush,*
> *Angie,*
> *you have no idea*
> *who he is.*
But my jaws
clamp.

"You're grumpy.
I'll call him,"
she offers
and digs out
a sparkly blue cell phone.

Well why not?
She's already more a part of my family
than I am.

She gets his answering service.

"No, no, his mom invested in that waterfront
    thing and now it's belly-up.
They already took out, like, a second mortgage
    on the house.
My mom knows the real estate broker.
I mean it.
Jed's family is flat broke."
Cherry-blossom lip gloss glues Marci's mouth
    into a smirk.

I am at the next table
shielded by a forkful of spaghetti special
and an escaped swath of hair.

Jed is broke?
He's always buying one of the guys a Coke,
gas for someone's car,
the latest music.

I glance around
and there's Jed at the back

listening to a buddy tell a story.
A slight smile on his lips
but a faraway look.

I'm staring.

Because isn't it incredible,
how you don't know much
about the people you spend every day with.

Watching mom's hair curl
in the steam from the broth,
biting my upper lip.

I offer my pyramid of meatballs
and finally stutter,
"Would you,
maybe,
come to
my game
Friday?"

Distracted in her timing
she sighs,
"Oh, I don't know.
Fridays are so busy."

I back away,
sandpaper mouth,
stumbling in my newly enlarged feet,
grasping the table

smeared with raw meat.

Right.

Mom is usually
home alone
on Friday nights.

I think
of mom as an oasis,
center of calm
in raging rapids.

But what a deception

because if I tread water in that spot
with her too long
I am lulled in froth,
mesmerized,
brain waves whirlpooled
to stay there
too,

watching petals
feathers
branches
whirl by.

Why does she stay there?

Saturday night,
dejected in the dark,
dancing halfheartedly with an embarrassingly
  eager guy
      a full head shorter than me,
      his body gyrating with abandon,
when I finally catch sight of Kyler
leaning on the wall near the front speakers.

This is terrible.
How do I nonchalantly happen to go by him
  when he's standing so far from any
  path of travel?
Has he been there all night?
Harvest Dance is already more than half over.
Maybe he changed his mind,
he's staying out of the way.
      Maybe I should just slink out the back at
        the end of this stupid, endless song,
            right about now.
Maybe—

Wait.

He's pushing off the wall,
heading right for me!

The heavy beat of the song fades,
my own internal beat heating up.

Eager Short Kid slugs me in the arm,
"Hey, how 'bout another one?"
I think I murmur no thanks,
pushing through people toward the smile on
   Kyler's lips.

Taking both my arms in his hands,
he laughs,
"An opening at last!
You are a popular girl!"

I open my mouth to protest
that I was just biding time waiting for him,

but in my wisest decision to date,
I close my mouth again
as he pulls me in for what happens to be a
slow
song.

Swaying,
>   turning in that
>>   slow
>   dance
circle.

My heart thumping,
or his?

It seems the same rhythm,
chest to chest,
my cheek at the bottom of his jaw.

If it's my heartbeat
I need to slow it down,
seem relaxed.

If it's his heartbeat,
he's as excited as I am to be dancing together,
and I am thrilled by this,
and nervous

that he's nervous.
He smoothes his hands over my lower back.

And then I feel it.

Our legs are the same length
so our hips are the same height.

I feel it,
panic,
try to pull away just enough so I'm not
   pressed up against it
without being too obvious.

Kyler pulls back a little too—
now we're both
embarrassed.

At the end of the song I chirp "Thanks!"
running for the safety of the girls' room.

What did that mean?

Doesn't an erection
mean
he wants to have sex?

I don't know him enough for that.

Dammit.

I liked him so much before this happened.
He's warm,
       like buttered pancakes and bacon
         snuggled on the plate,
       like a Synchilla jacket in the frost of
         morning,
       like the scent of cedar smoke from a
         chimney.

But this other thing.

I don't know how to put them together in the
    same person
and still like him.

Last to shower
Sunday morning,
who knows where my family disappeared to.

There's a note for me to do laundry.

Yay.

It's going to take more than stinky clothes
to wipe my mind of Ky—
        don't even think his name.

Banging around the kitchen,
I finally throw down a handful
   of Oat Crunchers,
        wonder what he eats for breakfast—
        don't—
and munching loudly,
pound downstairs to start the
   washing machine.

My knee pads are still wet

on top of the dryer
so I toss them in even though heat'll
    kill elastic—
            Kyler elastic—
            DON'T—
and I press the button,
lean against the rumbling metal,
listening to the *kathunka-thunka* of two knee
    pads making the rounds.

Going to be a long day

and I'm already sick of myself.

Amazing
how you can spend so much of the school day
hoping
to see someone,

and when things go wrong
how you can spend so much of the school day
desperate
to avoid them.

Kyler is watching me
as I am trapped in the lunch line—
        please don't talk to me
        please don't talk to me
—his eyes full of hurt,
and I feel bad,
but it's so much easier
when Rona arrives and cuts in front of me
so I have someone to yell at,
joke too loudly with,
shove around,
and I don't have to look at his eyes.

He actually comes to my locker.
"Can I please talk to you for a minute?"
Kyler's face is squinched up.

I feel my face go white and paper thin
as I nod,
and he takes my elbow
        in a gentle, nice way,
moving us around a corner to the back
   stairwell.

All I can think of is
this is where couples kiss,
but that is so obviously not
   what he wants right now.

He lets go of my elbow,
grasps my hand just for a second and
releases it,
a trace of a grimace.

He leans against the wall

with a whoosh of breath,
rubbing the sleek part of his neck with a
    long hand,
and looks up at me from a ducked head—
"I'm sorry."

I feel my jaw drop.
"I'm the one who ran," I retort.

He smirks a little.
"I don't blame you.
I just like you so much and—and—and—
I don't seem to have a lot of control over what
    that, um, does to me."

His widened pupils flicker from the floor to me
    and back again.
I blush.

"I just like you, Anke.
I just want to do stuff together sometimes,

maybe.
We like the same things, like hiking."

"So we could be . . . good friends, then,"
   I manage to say.

"Yeah!" he says with a relieved grin,
and I am angry at myself   for saying it,
and disappointed in him   for agreeing.

At the beginning of the night
my father put on his horrible mask
and made me hide behind him in the doorway
so I could see
their little terrified faces
and trembling bags of goodies.
"Trick or treat?"

He was unrelenting,
not saying a word,
just breathing,
     a beast smelling carrion.

Several ran away without candy
causing him
great glee.

Then he got bored
closed the door,
one naked outside bulb on,

and played the recording
of wolves howling

and no one came
after that.

"What if he died?"
Words bounce off the wall, the dryer,
   the concrete floor,
land with a *poof* in the pile of laundry
   we're folding.

Yaicha swings to stare at me in shock.
"I can't believe you'd even say
that
out loud."
She whispers like he's in the next room.

I shrug,
for once looking her in the eye.
"So. What if he did?"

Her lashes sweep down.
"It's not going to happen."

I'm feeling ruthless.
"Just go with it."

I blow my hair forcefully out of my vision.
"What if he died?"

The whites of her eyes show
so that her irises seem very small,
       like a cartoon character who realizes
       they've just stepped off the cliff of the
             Grand Canyon.
"Tell me you aren't going to try and—
and—
kill him," she hisses.

She is so out there.
"I said 'died,' Yaicha, not 'I'm going to kill him.'
  Think about it. What would we do?"

She breathes hard through her nose,
then turns away,
picks up her stack of laundry
in a sweep of sudden washerwoman authority.
"Only the good die young.
He'll live to be a hundred and twenty."

Stretching on the living room floor
contorting myself
to relax my left gluteus minimus.

Switching legs,
my head is almost under
his chair.

I start to scootch away,
then stop,
noticing upholstery staples in a line
under the seat.

One is loose.

Reaching under,
I pick at it.

It's out.

Look, that one's loose, too.

It's out.

And another
and another
and one more

and the under-fabric is sagging.

Think I'm finished stretching.

Burst of energy—
scramble full tilt downstairs to the garage
to sprinkle
          staples
                    over cold fish bones
at the bottom of the trash can.

State Quarter Finals!
A home game!

Rona is always in uniform first,
running in and out
to warm up
and report who's arrived in the stands.

She trots in
with the update
of our fans.
"Jackie's mom,
Ellen's mom,
Irene's two hot brothers!"
and her eyes slide
over me.

"No one yet."

They won't come.

They never do.

My father
says
competition is bad

but in biology class
we talked about
how
without competition
there is no
natural selection
and
we all could have
died
out
because we didn't fight back
when some angry ape
slapped us around
or
pillaged our bananas.

Survival
depends on

contesting the despot,
competing for the best bananas,
fitness in the fight.

Works for me.
I am ready for the opposition.

We won the match in two games,
and I soared,
I soared!

I jumped so high,
tendons of steel,
I pounded that Molten right
  into the floorboards,

our home crowd was enormous,
stamping, yelling,

I was fierce,
a warrior,
dominant!
Dominant!

On to the semi-finals!

Afterward,
Coach raised an eyebrow.

"What got into you today?
Quite the performance."

Weird—
I am not sure,
but he seemed
a little
concerned.

Feeling out of sorts,
uneasy,
Sunday bluesy,
low-down,

and I shouldn't be, right?

Great volleyball on Friday night,
moving on to the semis—

but I am in a funk,
raking the last of the rain-mashed leaves,
watery snot dripping off my nose.

The bubble of game greatness has popped

and I am back to plain old me,
alone and soggy on the lawn,

a drizzle beginning to fall.

Thanksgiving is coming this month
and in some doomy-gloomy premonition
I feel like
I have nothing to be thankful for.

I am annoyed
in my underwear
when Angeline comes into the locker room
  before Monday's practice,
clutching her pale pink sweater,
breathlessly spilling
that we could pick up government law info
at my father's office.

"He said 'Sure!'" she squeals.

His specialty,
and grudgingly I am thinking it *would* help us
on Thursday, Government Day.
I grunt on my knee pads.

He'll leave a folder on his desk because,
sigh,
"he might have a meeting."
She is briefly bereft.

I say I'll meet her in the lobby after practice.

"Oh, I told him I'd go, I don't mind."

Grrrr.
He *is my* father.
"No, I'll meet you," I throw at her
retreating back
but she's gone.

Cock my foot to lace my left sneaker.

"Why don't you just frickin' move in with us,"
  I say out loud.

I'll be glad when this government thing is over,
this annoying extracurricular supposed honor
that forces me to spend
even more time
with Angeline.

I'm a little late
getting to my father's building
after hanging out in the locker room
   with Rona, reliving every play
   from the Quarters
             and making up a few.
I scan for Angeline in the lobby
then sprint up the three flights
             on postpractice elation's momentum.
Coming to the Dr. Larus Feld etched on his
   frosted door,
I hitch up my sweatpants,
hoping he's not in.

Tapping lightly,
turning the knob,
the door swings in silence, fangs of light
   glinting in the glass.

Then I hear—

I hear—something—soft crying somewhere.

Angeline?

> Clamping gym bag to my body,
> sneakers on carpet,
>> carpet,
>> carpet,
> lean around the bookcase—

My
father with a small smile
leaning toward the armchair,
zipper on its way down,
Angeline, her skirt tweaked,
swelling closing one eye,
pleading softly, no, no,

"NO!"
Dr. Feld is shock still.
I take another lungful,

"NO!"
　　　　Angie slides to standing,
　　　　gathering her book bag,
　　　　running for the exit.
Raising brows, he mocks me,
but, dammit, he will hear me,

"NO!"

Slamming by the bookcase
tearing through the doorway
pounding down the stairwell,
no-no-no-no,
NO-NO-NO.

She is gone when I get outside,
so I'm running toward home
along the railroad tracks,
gym bag whacking my back,
not smelling the oily rails,
crows muted,
sun dim,
tunnel vision only two feet
in front of my feet,

my only companion
that shrill pitch above me,
the one they use
in movies
when something terrible is revealed.

Throwing my gym bag down
by the brook
with a crunch of fine ice,
I double over,
dry heaves
on my knees.

What did I see?
What did I see in his office?

How could he, to
poor Angeline?

I sink onto a rock near the water,
taking a blood-red
maple leaf
and dunking it under,
holding it beneath the frigid liquid.

Poor Angie.

She was supposed to be outside our

house of horrors
and I let her in.
I should have kept her away from him.
He went outside.

And the tears burst through
heavy as mercury,
heated by guilt,
and I take the leaf out of the water,
sobbing.

Angeline,
Angie,
I'm sorry.

Trudging
trudging up the driveway,
patches of ice,
Darren sweeping
patches of wood chips.

"Go look out back,"
he says with a jerk of his head,
stamping the broom,
and I am
standing,
staring . . .

"Go look," he says.

. . . then trudging
past,
saying nothing,
peeling my coat
to cool myself down.

From the dining room
I gape at the backyard,
suddenly so vast and bright
even in twilight,

the old hemlock tree gone.

Stump and sawdust.
Cut off at the knees.

"It had that disease,"
Mom says,
"it might have spread.
The tree had to go."

I flash with incendiary anger at her.
Then, pressing my forehead
to the chilled glass of the sliding door,
an ice block

forms in my chest.

My climbing tree.
My pinecone supply.
My hiding spot in the middle of the yard.
Gone.

Pushing open the bathroom door
I take two steps toward Yaicha
who is wrestling with her hair.

"I saw him hurt Angeline."

The brush stops moving.

"At his office today."

Small sounds
        like a dying cricket
come from Yaicha's lips.
"I'm sure you were mistaken," she says
   to her brush.

My ears pin back—
"MISTAKEN?
I know who Angie is, Yaicha.
I know who our father is, Yaicha.
He hurts people, he hurts you,

you never do anything!"
My claws scrape the wall paint.

She turns with soft rabbit eyes.
"He'll kill me."

"He's already doing that!"
I am growling, grabbing her sleeve,
"Every day,
every day he rips you open,
chips off pieces week by week,
till a few years from now you are not even a
   mouthful of sawdust.
A drawn-out killing.
Well, I'm tired of all of us doing nothing.
He has to be stopped."

Yaicha's eyes have flinched a few times
but soften again.
"Nobody can stop him."

My teeth show.

"Nobody can stop him?
Good.
To him I have always been
Nobody."

"No-no-no-no, Anke,
What're you going to do . . . ?"
Yaicha is whispering, pleading.

I storm outside
to visit the stump
and hear her hammer downstairs and streak
 out the garage to tell Darren.
In a weird echo along the hedge
I hear him say,
"No, she can't. . . .
Let's talk to mom."

And in the gathering night
I stand on dying chips,
stare at the new cut
oozing plasma,
sticky,
drying in the chill.

The family secret,

carefully contained for years,
out in the open air.

Now Yaicha and Darren are talking to mom
in the living room.

I hear his car
slow for the gravel turn
at the bottom of the driveway
and I head
inside.

Where is the safe, cuddling daddy
who
sang "I'm Being Swallowed by a Boa
    Constrictor" to me

                    when I had a fever?

Was that man molted off
like scales that no longer
lie smoothly
around the shape of what he has become?

I want my daddy back.

Too bad for me.

PART
FOUR

They all swivel to me—
Mom, Darren, and Yaicha—
as I come through the sliding door.
Mom's mouth opens
then closes
when the garage door
goes up.

Then comes down.

Footfall,
Darren frozen, eyes on the baseboard,
Yaicha melted against the stereo cabinet,
as he steps lightly up the stairs.

"Sorry I couldn't give you
a ride home,"
he says to me,
sliding into the living room
with his briefcase,

"I had a meeting."

His eyes dare me.

Dare me.

Slow   motion

twitching

        twitching

                hissing burning

                blood pushing

                itching skin

                        pushing out

                        something scary

                        pushing out

                        something stronger.

I stand behind his chair.
"Liar,"

      under my breath.

      His eyebrows rise,
      pupils sharpen.

"You weren't at a meeting,"
      take a breath, gain speed, bursting,
"You were with Angie in the office.
I saw you. I saw you.
You clamp us down,
you think no one knows.
You hurt my brother! My sister!
You hurt my friend! Small trusting prey, huh?
You had to squash some weak person
  already in pain,
      thinking she loved you.
You could have chosen to hurt *me*!

But I'm not worth enough I never am and
   you picked poor Angie,
   you were going to RAPE her,
   I SAW YOU TRY TO RAPE ANGIE,
   you fucking MONSTER!"

      I shove his chair forward
      with the force of my words,
      the wooden leg touches
      his foot.

      Stillness. Shaking.

      White-faced, cold,
      slowly
      he picks it up by the seat.

      Suddenly spinning the chair in air
      he smashes it on me

hard—

with a great crack
I go down,
splinters of wood
splinters of bone
my leg showing bone,

and finally
I
roar.

Coming out of anesthesia,
throwing up
as the doctor
explains
one rod, two plates, eight screws
he planted
in my leg bone.
A recipe for repair.

"No duct tape?" I croak.

Leaning off the hospital bed,
convulsing again.
Throwing up
feels
strangely
good.

In the sweeping blur
the doctor's

purple high-tops
swim into focus.

I can barely hear his grin.

"Nope, no duct tape."

The teeny card attached
        with a green Band-Aid on a heart
says *from*
Coach Roy and Rona and the Team
in florist script.

An arrangement bursting
with
stripy-throated trumpety flowers
the exact color of
salmon sashimi.
        Alstroemeria, Mom called them.

I am grinning.

My team.

My first real bouquet.

Mom perches
on the gurney edge,
flicking, straightening the beautiful
one perfect
flame-colored rose
she brought.

"I threw him out, Anke.
Out."

Softly, fiercely,
she rips a petal.

He's been arrested.

In jail.

Such an odd disconnect

to feel so relieved
and so guilty,

yet so cold about the whole thing,
like concrete,
like a nuclear reactor decommissioned
    and left by itself to withstand the
        winter.

I wonder if he has to wear one of those
  bar-striped suits.

I scootch up straighter.
Mom props pillows
and then they stand there,

Mom, stroking my hair,
Darren, staring at me
      like he suddenly sees my eyes are brown,
Yaicha, wearing pink, squeezing my toes,
      looking at me,
      then out the hospital window.

I am
grateful they came,
embarrassed they wanted to.

I want hugs,
I want
to ask them to leave,
but when they finally go
I am lonely
again.

I can't be
still
in this antiseptic bed.

I knock my new
shocking green cast
against the metal rails
even though it hurts
to do it,
rocking my leg
        back and forth, *whack*
        back and forth, *whack*
        back and forth, *whack*.

I did it.

        back and forth, *whack*

I filed
a restraining order
against

my own father.

    back and forth, *whack*

He's out on bail
and needs more than restraining.

    back and forth, *whack*, ***WHACK***.

But it's
a damn good
start,
and

I did it.

Angeline has a lawyer

and
I have a doctor
and
       strong pain medication
       for where my bone
       punched through to the open air,
       a desperate method
       of escape,
       and I'm a little proud of it.

Angie has a therapist
too

and
they want one for me.

But I told them I need
to think on my own
first.

I am staring at the nothingness of the
    hospital room
when a fluttering of yellow
catches my eye.

Long fingers curve around the door frame
waving a birch leaf.

I prop myself,
grinning,
wondering.
"Hello?" I call.

Blond hair and one crinkled light brown eye
    show next to the doorjamb,
then the rest of Kyler's smiling face.

"Hey," he says gently.

"Hey!" I say,

my heart skipping up in tempo.

Stepping into the room,
Kyler reaches gingerly into the chest pocket of
  his flannel shirt,
drawing out a handful of autumn leaves.

"For me?" I say gleefully,
palms up for him to lay them on.

He sits easily on the side of the bed,
watching me go through beech, oak, maple.

"I didn't know your favorite flower," he says,
like it's an apology.

I raise the pile of leaves and breathe
  their scent,
looking up into Kyler's eyes.

"These *are* my favorite," I say.

Lying spread eagle,
anchored
by my leg cast
to the driveway
    still barely warm
    from an unseasonal day.

Staring into the starred darkness
makes me feel
stronger,
a simple truth.

With all the
dizzy galaxies
    hot gases
        dust at the speed of light
           neutrinos running through
           everything,

no matter how powerful someone is
    here on Earth

they are just as small as me
to the vast greatness of
outer
space.

Strangely calm
about missing the State Semi-Finals.

We lost.

It's too bad,
but I secretly feel kind of proud
that maybe we lost
because
I wasn't there.

And I'll be back next year.

An envelope
under my door
in the morning.

Anke,
in my mother's
small script.

Inside, a love letter:

> I am sorry I let you down.
> Your strength has always been immense,
> I think I believed your father
> needed me more.
> He is in such pain, and I chose not to
>   see some things he did to feel better.
> Shielded by my love for him,
> I always did what I thought was best
> for my marriage—
> I see I failed you, my daughter.
> I sacrificed my children.
> Please help me

be a better mother to you now.
I love you, I need you.

And I am crying
stumping out to the hall
enveloping Mom in a smothering of
  pajama arms,
pounding her shoulder with my fist,
pounding,
damn you,
mingling tears,
I love you, too.

I wish I could ask Yaicha
what it was like
what she was thinking
what she was feeling
what made her lie still
while he hurt her so badly.

I wish I could
but I don't know how to bring up
such horrible questions.

Maybe they are none of my business.

Maybe she is wanting someone to ask.

Do I just open my mouth over homework,
brushing teeth,
folding laundry?
Do I just plunk myself on the edge of her bed
   one morning
and ask?

I find myself crying all the time—
right now,
for instance.

It comes over me at the weirdest moments,
like boiling water for tea
or chopping wood for the fire.

At first I thought it was just leftover reaction.

But I feel like I'm breaking into a thousand
    random pieces, unsolvable.

And Darren is at the door of my bedroom
with a sad face,
and he comes and puts his arm around me—I
    can't remember when he's ever done that—

and I realize he loves me maybe and I haven't
    ruined the whole family and ripped us all
    to shreds and maybe they don't hate me and
    it'll be okay and now I'm crying even harder,
    sobbing on Darren,
    holding him around his neck
    like I'm ten years old,
    and he says
"Add some soap, you'd be a great washing
    machine."
and I am laughing and crying and I am so glad
    I have my brother.

The turkey seems way too big this year.

Did just one person
take up
that much table?

The steam leaks from a vent in the crackly skin
just like a touched-up photo
in *Chef's Fare*.
But we are not in a magazine.

I thought maybe
we'd all know what we're thankful for.
He's *gone*, isn't he?

It was Yaicha's idea.
Mom said,
"Just the chair!"
and something about pumpkin pie having gone
   to our heads.

But Darren finds a broken crate,
leftover shingles,
a branch of cedar,
to jumpstart the bonfire,

so our father's teak armchair
will really burn,
burn completely away.

The fire howls to life,
cedar sap snapping,
and when it is so hot
we have to shield our faces,
Darren helps me throw on the chair,
upholstery down,
shattered frame to the blackening sky,

flames lapping
three unbroken legs
     awkward in the air.

The three of us let out a cheer
dancing, me stumping, in a crazy circle
fed by the blaze,

and Yaicha sings,
"Ding-dong, the wicked witch is dead!"

And then the silliness stops.
Yaicha
Darren
and I
are standing
with our scarves to our noses,
saying nothing
thinking everything
eyes glued to the pulsing core of the fire.

I nudge
a burning twig with my toe,
reflecting
on my father himself.
I have loved him,
feared him,
loathed him,
for so long.

But what does he have
to give me

now
that I would actually want?

The final chair leg tumbles
to the coals,

and I can't come up with
one
thing.

Yaicha and I
sit against the big hemlock stump
heads nearly touching
through the feathery needled sprout
between us.

Darren is silhouetted,
standing,
arms folded,
facing the fire.

"Come sit with us,"
I tell him,
patting the ground
like he's a small child.

And he comes!
He sits on my other side,
arm around the scratchy bark,

throwing tiny chips into the coals.

Three of us,
facing the embers,
leaning on the scent
of fresh-sawn wood.

They head into the house,
Darren patting my shoulder,
Yaicha touching my hair.

Resting my cast on a smoldering shingle
I stare into coals,
eyelids drying,
small pulsing flames emblazoned on my vision
   when I finally blink.

I shiver
with contrasts
like the planet Mercury,
      one side boiling
      one side frozen

and here I am crying again
because that sounds so lonely,
I am tired of
being lonely,
so done with

being lonely.

And yes!

I *am* done with being lonely
because there,
sticking their heads out the sliding-glass door
are my mother,
my brother,
my sister,
calling me
    "Come in!"
        "It's cold out there alone!"
            "We're making hot chocolate!"

Wrapped in a grin,
I douse the last embers
and turn on my cast
away from ashes.

Toward offered afghan.
Toward mug of frothy warmth.
Toward my family.

ACKNOWLEDGMENTS

I thank the following people for jumping on the
furniture with me:

My agent, Ginger Knowlton

My editor, Catherine Frank

The Fairy GodSisters, Ink, of Santa Barbara

(Lee, Robin, Val, and Mary)

The Ventura Group for Wayward Writers

(Lynn, Laura, Dan, and Siri)

The Divine Keri Collins

Styliani Munroe, niece of extraordinary and

much-appreciated enthusiasm

Jon Chinburg, a sweet boy from down the street

and a sweet man now

and

Sonya Sones, for her belief in the importance of this

novel at a very early stage